FLOWER FAIRY STORY-BOOKS

A MIDWINTER TALE

Fay Marden

Illustrated by Elsa Godfrey

Based on The Flower Fairies
created by Cicely M Barker

Blackie

Do you believe in fairies?

I hope you do, for believe me, they are everywhere about – in the hedgerow, a pretty garden or a shady woodland glade. Who knows? There may be fairies working in your garden while you sit and read this book. Just imagine that!

Flower fairies are the most enchanting little creatures you have ever seen but it would not surprise me if you had *never* seen them, for they are such timid folk, they hide themselves away. It is their job to look after all the lovely things growing in the world, for every tree or flower belongs to a flower fairy or an elf. Did you know that?

No? Then I have so many stories to tell you. Listen, and I will tell you a story about winter and how the flower fairies helped someone in need.

It all began one cold midwinter morning. The Holly Pixie was the first to wake. He uncurled himself from his prickly bed and peeped over a cluster of bright red berries. Then his eyes grew wide with amazement.

'Snow!' he cried. 'Look at the snow!'

Sure enough, snow had fallen in the night and the Fairy Dell was covered in a thick blanket of white. It was an enchanting sight.

One by one all the fairy folk began to stir. Elves and pixies jumped out of bed and ran to their windows.

'Come out and play!' called the Holly Pixie. 'It's such fun!'

Soon the Dell was full of jolly folk, warmly dressed in hats and scarves, slipping and sliding all over the place. Even the little woodmice awoke from their slumbers to join in the fun.

'Oh, Lavender, isn't it pretty?' said Poppy, who had just peeped out of her door and had seen Lavender skip by. But before Lavender had time to reply . . . Whooosh! A snowball landed at her feet.

'Ooo!' cried Lavender. 'Who did that?'

She turned and saw Holly peeping round the trunk

of a tree. He looked rather red in the face.

'I'm sorry, Lavender,' he said. 'I didn't mean to throw it at you. That snowball was meant for Thistle but he ducked down behind a bush.'

'That's all right,' laughed Lavender. 'But watch where you're aiming next time!'

The two fairies were still laughing when suddenly, there came the sound of excited voices and squeals of delight. Four baby elves had made a toboggan from an old, dry chestnut leaf and were sliding down a steep hill.

'Hold on tight!' called Poppy, anxiously.

'Mind the holly tree!' warned Lavender, as the toboggan sped towards it.

Too late. Four baby elves, toboggan and all went swish
. . . swish . . . BUMP! right into the middle of the
prickly holly.

'Ouch, ooo, ow!' wailed the four baby elves. Poppy
and Lavender had to run to their rescue and pick them
out of the holly one by one.

'Dear me, dear me,' said Mother Elf as she came out
to see what all the fuss was about. The baby elves were
covered in prickly holly leaves and were crying bitterly.

Then the Holly Pixie arrived.

'Look what you've done to my tree!' he scolded.

'Hmph!' said Mother Elf indignantly. 'Never mind
about your tree, Master Holly. Look what *it's* done to
my children!'

And with that, Mother Elf marched her four babies
off to bathe their wounds and give them mugs of hot
blackberry juice and honey.

'Well, I like that!' said Holly, shaking his fist after
Mother Elf.

'Don't be cross,' laughed Poppy. 'Your tree hasn't
really come to much harm and the baby elves are safe
and well. Come on, let's fly to the edge of the wood and
look at the snow.'

'May I come, too?' called a tiny voice. It was dear
little Forget-me-not. She had heard the baby elves
crying and had come to see what was the matter.

'Of course you can,' said Lavender. She took the
little fairy by the hand and together they flew with the
others to the edge of the wood.

In autumn, long before the cold winter winds had come
and long before the first snowflake had fallen in the
Fairy Dell, swallows had gathered to fly far away to the
warm summer sun of the South.

But one poor bird had injured its wing and could
not fly as fast as the others and in time they had flown
away, leaving him at the edge of the wood. Poor thing!
Imagine how miserable he must have been. The injured
bird had taken shelter beneath a bush and there he had
stayed for many weeks, feeding himself as best as he
could. Now the first snow had fallen and he was weak
and hungry and very, very cold.

That morning, by chance, Holly, Poppy, Lavender
and Forget-me-not flew down close to the very spot

where the bird lay freezing in the snow. At first, the swallow was startled by their excited chatter but he, like all other creatures, knew that fairy folk were good and kind to animals and that if he could only make them hear, they might be able to help him.

'Look!' cried Poppy, pointing to the snow piled high against the hedges. 'It looks like whipped cream,' said the Holly Pixie. 'Yum, yum!'

'Can't you think of anything but food!' laughed Lavender.

Only little Forget-me-not was silent. For above the fairy voices, she alone had heard something else. A cry so weak and thin that she knew at once it was the sound of someone in need.

'Listen,' she said, 'I can hear someone calling.'

The four friends listened carefully. Yes, there it was again, a faint *peep – peep – peep*!

'Over there,' whispered Holly, pointing to a bush.

And there they found the swallow, still alive but very weak.

'We must help him at once,' said Poppy. 'Holly, go quickly and collect some of your best and juiciest berries. The poor creature must be starving.'

'Of course,' said Holly and he dashed off straightaway.

Lavender bent down and saw that the swallow's wing was broken.

'We must find the Self-heal Fairy. She will know what to do,' she said.

'I'll go,' said Poppy and flew off to look for her.

Then, while Lavender gently brushed the snow away and made the poor swallow as comfortable as she could, little Forget-me-not sat close by and sang him a fairy lullaby. The swallow opened his eyes.

'Thank you,' he whispered. 'As soon as my wing is mended, I will get my strength back, you'll see!'

'Hush now,' said Lavender. 'You must rest and sleep and wait for the others to come.'

'I do wish they would hurry,' sighed Forget-me-not, gently stroking the swallow's head. And she put her tiny arms around his breast and hugged him close to keep him warm.

When Poppy and Holly reached the Dell everyone wanted to help. The Self-heal Fairy was soon found and she gathered together her basket of herbs and medicines. Six strong pixies plaited some beech twigs to make a bed and Mother Elf gave them a snug feather quilt to keep the swallow warm.

Meanwhile, the Holly Pixie had collected some of his very best berries and soon he and all the others were ready to make their way through the wood to where Lavender and Forget-me-not were waiting. When the fairy folk arrived all their anxious little faces peered down at the injured creature.

The Self-heal Fairy stepped forward and smiled at Forget-me-not, whose eyes were filled with tears.

'Don't cry,' she said gently. 'You must help me now by talking to the swallow while I mend his wing. That is most important.'

So, while Self-heal set to work, Forget-me-not sat and comforted the bird so that he should not be frightened. When Self-heal had bound the broken wing with her bandage of fine web, she beckoned to Holly.

'You may give him two, small ripe berries,' she said, 'then we must take him back to the Dell.'

Now, fairy folk are such small creatures that the swallow was really quite large by comparison, and it took six pixies and three fairies to wrap him gently in the quilt and lift him on to the bed of twigs. Then slowly they carried him along the woodland path. By now it was late afternoon and growing dark, so that the little procession had to find its way by the light of the moon. How clear and bright it shone on the cold, white snow!

At last, they arrived back safely in the Dell. Mother Elf had found a cosy place where the fairies could look after the sick bird – a hollow at the foot of an oak tree. She had swept it clean and had made a nest of sweet-smelling heather and thyme.

All through the night, the fairies took it in turns to sit near the hollow. Only little Forget-me-not insisted on curling herself up and sleeping by the swallow's side. All the next day he slept, waking only to take some nourishing food and to allow the Self-heal Fairy to smooth his wing with ointment.

And so the days went by until . . . one morning, when all the fairy folk were fast asleep, they were awoken by the happiest sound of all.

'*Chirrup, chirrup, chirrup, cheep!*'

Self-heal's medicines had worked and all the fairies' love and kindness had made the swallow strong and well again.

'Thank you, thank you, thank you!' he chirruped, so that everyone rushed to the hollow to see him.

'I feel well enough to fly!' sang the swallow, happily, but Self-heal was quick to make sure that he did no such thing.

'You must rest for some time yet,' she said. 'Your wing is not yet mended. I am afraid you will have to be patient.'

The days that followed were happy days for the little bird, for although his own family were far away, the fairies and elves were his constant companions. How they all fussed and spoiled him!

But his dearest friend was Forget-me-not, who sat with him day after day, singing her songs and listening to stories of his travels to the warm countries of the South.

Then one day, Self-heal came and told Swallow that he was well enough to fly. She took the bandage from his wing and watched as he stretched it out and settled the feathers smoothly in place.

'Thank you,' he said. 'You have been a wonderful doctor. I cannot thank you enough and I have nothing to give you in return.'

'Making you strong and well is reward enough,' smiled Self-heal.

'But tomorrow night is our Christmas Party and there *is* something rather special you can do for us all . . .' And Self-heal smiled again as she whispered something in his ear.

The following day, the Dell was full of excited fairy folk busily preparing for the party. The baby elves were hanging boughs of holly round the Dell, only this time they were very careful not to get themselves stuck on the prickles!

Poppy and Lavender ran in and out of the trees, weaving ribbons of ivy and hanging fairy lanterns on the boughs. And all the while, fairies and pixies ran to and fro, carrying plates of delicious things to eat and jugs full of elderberry wine and tansy pop.

And in the midst of it all stood the lovely Christmas Tree, twinkling with a hundred silver stars. It was a magical sight.

By evening, everything was ready. The fairies had dressed themselves in their very best party dresses and the pixies were as clean and tidy as could be expected. Even the baby elves were there and on their best behaviour!

Everyone gathered round the Christmas Tree for they were waiting for someone rather special to arrive. Can you guess who that special someone might have been? Why, the Christmas Fairy, of course!

Suddenly, from high above the trees, came the sound of tiny tinkling bells and as everyone gazed upwards, they saw a sight to fill their hearts with joy and gladness on that Christmas night. It was none other than their own dear swallow, swooping down towards them with the Christmas Fairy on his back. And there, too, sat little Forget-me-not, jingling a circlet of bells for all to hear.

How gracefully the swallow landed and set the fairies down! How all the fairy folk cheered to see him fly! Then the moment they had all been waiting for – the Christmas Fairy opened a silver sack and gave a special little parcel to each and every one. And to the swallow, she gave a tiny silver harebell to wear around his neck, so that he should remember them always.

'I shall never forget you,' said the gentle bird. 'You have all been so kind, especially you, dear Forget-me-not. You are well-named and I shall return each spring to see you all, I promise.'

And the swallow kept his promise.

In fact, each and every spring you will see swallows returning after the long cold winter months have passed. Who knows, the very first swallow you see in your garden next spring, may be the very one that Forget-me-not knew and loved so well.

The Flower Fairies copyright © The Estate of Cicely M Barker
1923, 1925, 1926, 1934, 1940, 1944, 1948
Text copyright © Fay Marden 1986
Illustrations copyright © Elsa Godfrey 1986

First published 1986 by
Blackie and Son Ltd
7 Leicester Place, London WC2H 7BP

British Library Cataloguing in Publication Data
Marden, Fay
  A midwinter tale.—(Flower fairies story books)
  I. Title   II. Godfrey, Elsa   III. Barker,
  Cicely Mary   IV. Series
  823'.914[J]   PZ7

  ISBN 0-216-91982-7

Printed in Great Britain by
Holmes McDougall Limited, Edinburgh